This Walker book belongs to :

_____

_____

_____

For Elizabeth
and Lucy

First published 1988 by Walker Books Ltd
87 Vauxhall Walk, London SE11 5HJ

This edition published in 2008

2 4 6 8 10 9 7 5 3 1

This book has been typeset in Plantin.

Printed in China

British Library Cataloguing in Publication Data:
a catalogue record for this book
is available from the British Library.

ISBN 978-1-4063-1613-1

www.walkerbooks.co.uk

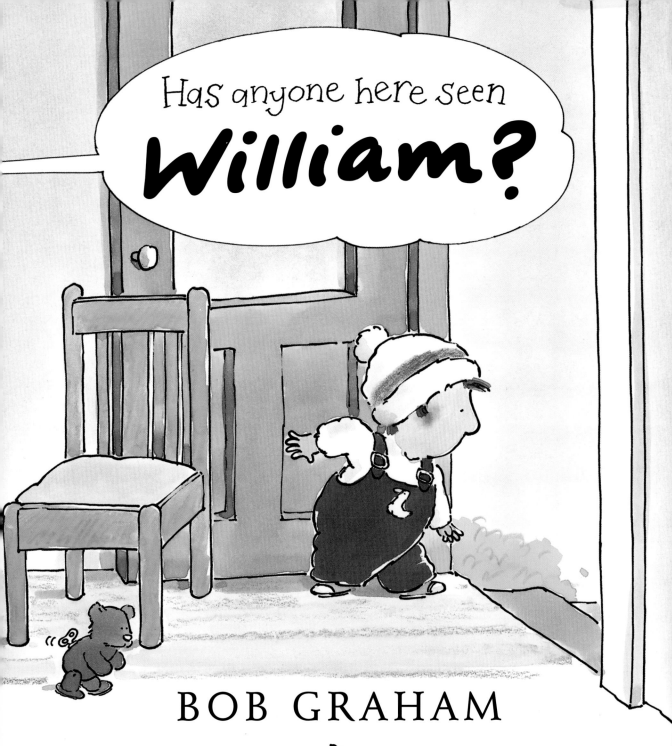

BOB GRAHAM

WALKER BOOKS
AND SUBSIDIARIES
LONDON · BOSTON · SYDNEY · AUCKLAND

Nobody saw William's first step.

It was straight into mid-air. He rolled down the steps like a soft red rubber ball – followed by his wind-up bear.

"Where's your brother, Jeremy? Ruth? Alice?"

The bear now walked with a slight limp and often fell over.
So did William. Things had to be moved out of his reach.
The handles of pots were turned in and the curtains tied up.

But William's mum and dad sometimes forgot.
"Did you tie the curtains in the children's room, dear?"

Now that William was walking, he was just like his bear.

Wind him up and off he would go.
Nothing stopped him until the key ran out.

His sisters and brother did not always watch him.

Sooner or later someone would say...

Has anyone here seen William?

On his second birthday, William went shopping for a new shirt.

His patched and rusty bear went walking. So did William.

Suddenly William was gone. His mum ran frantically into the street.

That afternoon, there was a party with a special chocolate birthday cake for William.

"Keep a watch on William. He's been lost once today already."

"Time to eat," Mum said,
"and bring William with you."

Long after the party was over and the children had
been tucked up in bed,

and the dog had been put in her basket in the kitchen,

and all were asleep,
there was a noise downstairs.

Slowly, the kitchen door swung open…

and there was William!
The key in his old bear had made its last turn.

William had stopped too... at least until tomorrow.

BOB GRAHAM

Bob Graham is one of Australia's finest author-illustrators.
Winner of the Kate Greenaway Medal, Smarties Book Prize and CBCA
Picture Book of the Year, his stories are renowned for celebrating the magic
of everydayness. Bob says, *"I'd like reading my books to be a little like opening
a family photo album, glimpsing small moments captured from daily lives."*

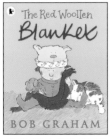

ISBN 978-1-4063-1649-0

ISBN 978-1-4063-1613-1

ISBN 978-1-4063-1647-6

ISBN 978-1-4063-1640-7

ISBN 978-1-4063-1648-3

ISBN 978-1-4063-1650-6

ISBN 978-0-7445-9827-8

WINNER OF THE CBCA PICTURE BOOK
OF THE YEAR AWARD (2002)

ISBN 978-1-4063-0851-8

WINNER OF THE
KATE GREENAWAY MEDAL (2002)

ISBN 978-1-84428-482-5

ISBN 978-1-4063-0132-8

ISBN 978-1-4063-0686-6

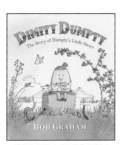

ISBN 978-1-84428-067-4

ISBN 978-1-4063-0338-4

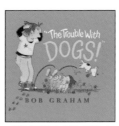

ISBN 978-1-4063-0716-0

ISBN 978-1-4063-1492-2

Available from all good bookstores

www.walkerbooks.co.uk
www.walkerbooks.com.au